Elizabeth Young

DUMP AND CHASE

Elizabeth Young teaches writing at Lesley University and Emmanuel College. She is currently working on her second novel. She lives near Boston with her husband, Michael Burtman and cat, Tim Thomas.

First published by GemmaMedia in 2012.

GemmaMedia
230 Commercial Street
Boston, MA 02109 USA

www.gemmamedia.com

Printed in the United States of America

16   15   14   13   12   1   2   3   4   5

978-1-936846-21-4

Library of Congress Cataloging-in-Publication Data

Young, Elizabeth, 1982–
    Dump and chase / Elizabeth Young.
        p. cm. — (Gemma open door)
    ISBN 978-1-936846-21-4
1. Young men—Fiction. 2. Hockey players—Fiction.
I. Title.
PS3625.O96417D86 2012
813'.6—dc23

                                    2012003743

Cover by Night & Day Design

Inspired by the Irish series of books designed for adult literacy, Gemma Open Door Foundation provides fresh stories, new ideas, and essential resources for young people and adults as they embrace the power of reading and the written word.

Brian Bouldrey
North American Series Editor

GEMMA
Open Door

Without taking his eyes off the television, Ken submerges his spoon in his cereal again. He comes up with a spoonful of milk. Two Rice Krispies remain, bloated and floating along opposite ends of the bowl.

He became so engrossed in this documentary that he's finished his breakfast without realizing it. He looks back to the television, to the documentary on beavers—a family of beavers building a dam with their human-like hands—and he decides he shouldn't stay tuned for the next segments on vegetation and flooding and hunting. How much does an ordinary man need to know about this, anyways?

He takes his bowl to the kitchen and

drains the milk over a fountain of dishes stuck to one another in the sink. Another week's worth of dishes, undone. He runs the water and thinks about how much he doesn't want to clean.

But today is Saturday, and on Saturdays he blasts his radio (WTRI, timeless soft rock) and vacuums the den, makes his bed, stain-sticks his clothes, and unsticks the dirty dishes in the sink. Then he showers, and shaves, and clips his toenails, and cuts his nose hairs, and spritzes his cologne, and hustles outside, where the latest model of Charger or Mustang or Roadster awaits him. (As the most senior Relations Associate of Rubble Rental, he always has his pick of the litter.) And, in his free rental, he visits the ATM to withdraw money, the liquor store to get a bottle of bubbly, the local supermarket to purchase a gift card, and then, finally, the condominium complex by the train tracks to pick up his girlfriend, Kendra (who also goes by Ken).

He thinks about the task before him as he stands over the kitchen sink, over the tower of dirty dishes. Today is not a good Saturday; he does not feel compelled to clean, and groom, and drive all across town. Today is one of those Saturdays when he is all too aware that he is forty-three years old, that he lives in a dirty apartment, that he doesn't really own a nice car, that he has attained his "Senior" Relations Associate title by being the oldest guy working behind the counter of Rubble Rental, and finally, that he dates a woman named Ken who is not really his girlfriend but a "girlfriend coach," which basically makes her an escort whom, on Saturdays, he takes to Bengy's Neighborhood Grille, then brings home for bubbly and a boinking, then pays with an American Express gift card.

He stacks his cereal bowl on top of the others in the kitchen sink and returns to his ratty couch and the beaver documentary.

By six o'clock, he has yet to dump his hamper into the washer. He has yet to shower, to shave, to clip his toenails, or to assess the length of his nose hairs. Instead, he tunes in for a music video marathon, and soon enough it is half past six. The fifteen minutes reserved for a shower have gone shamelessly to Beyoncé's short-shorts. Kendra won't mind if he smells like a hoagie.

Outside, he unlocks the forest green Mustang and ducks into the driver's seat. The fresh smell and the clean dash of the new car invigorate him; he feels better already.

He drives across town, over the hills and around tight bends, and he pretends he is Lieutenant Frank Bullitt, hot on the case. In actuality, he tails an unsuspecting Corolla, clearly marked T&S Driving School, and nearly follows the poor kid into the high school parking lot. Ken receives the nasty glare from the instructor, and he raises his palm as an apology.

He crosses the tracks, pulls into Kendra's condominium parking lot, and sighs. He wonders how she affords a condo, when he can barely make rent. There must be good money in girlfriend coaching. He pulls into the GUEST parking spot before her townhouse, unbuckles, checks his hair in the rearview again, and prepares to get out, hotfoot across the sidewalk and greet Kendra at her door, but she is already waiting for him outside the car.

She whips the passenger door open, ducks into the bucket seat and says, "Can we please not go to Bengy's?"

Ken has never known Kendra to be so forward. Her brashness causes him to pause. But he is further distracted by her hair. She wears her orange hair (a color that surely comes in a box) in a high ponytail, and he realizes that he has never seen her ears. She has elfish ears, and she is that much more adorable to him.

"I'll go anywhere but Bengy's," she

says, reaching over her shoulder for her seat belt.

Ken thinks for a moment. He can't come up with a single restaurant other than Bengy's. He's been taking her to Bengy's for months now. He enjoys their soup and salad combo with the endless breadsticks.

"Don't you like anything else?" she asks, as if she can read his mind. "Rib eyes, sirloin, burgers, or chicken? And what are we listening to?"

Ken lunges for the radio dial and tunes away from timeless soft rock. "I don't know what that was," he says, and he questions the manhood of the last guy to drive this rental. He tunes to WHRY, Hairy 94 point 2, a hard rock station that allegedly puts hair on your chest, though it mostly attracts already-hairy men. "Why don't you pick the restaurant?" he asks, changing the subject a little too excitedly. "I'll go anywhere your heart desires."

She chooses the Stockbridge Tavern, which is a loud restaurant with a panorama of flat screens, an endless selection of draft beer, and a novel of a menu. Crowded places (especially those with younger, more handsome crowds) make him nervous. He slouches in the driver's seat and looks into his lap. He hasn't prepared for this. If only he had put on a better pair of jeans. If only he owned a better pair of jeans.

Kendra props her elbow on the passenger window and rests her temple in her palm. She looks tired, or upset, Ken can never tell the difference. If the Stockbridge will make her happy, he can brave the crowd.

TWO

The hostess's podium is busy with a swarm of patrons grumbling curses and elbowing each other when they check their watches. Across the way, the bartender yells out to Ken and waves. For a moment, Ken believes he is suddenly popular, but the young man with nice thick hair scoffs at Ken and lowers his hand from the air. He is a friend of Kendra, and that is precisely why she and Ken are seated immediately—well before the angry and hypoglycemic hordes cursing out the hostess.

Ken and Kendra share a spacious booth just before the most massive flat screen, and Kendra, with her back to the television, cranes to view the Bruins game. He thinks of telling her how rude she's being. After all, if he were transfixed by the TV, she would correct him. As his girlfriend coach, she teaches him how to be polite to his date. She teaches him how to compliment and how to properly accept a compliment. She teaches him how to start a conversation and how to tactfully back out of an inappropriate conversation inadvertently started. And she teaches him how *not* to space out and stare at her chest while she's talking, though he desperately wants to.

He plucks two breadsticks from the

basket and tells her that she's breaking one of her own rules.

She turns to face him again and sighs. "It's the playoffs, Ken."

He butters one of the breadsticks before chomping on it. "Should that matter?"

"Don't talk with your mouth full. And yes," she says, "certain games are exempt from 'Rule 27: Attention must not be paid to television programs during dinner.'"

"I didn't know that."

"It's in the handbook. Addendum 27.1 finds television programs, including commercials, to be potential conversation starters in the event of awkward silence, which has happened here," she says, tapping her forefinger on the table.

"Furthermore, 27.2 clearly states that certain games, including any postseason NFL game, any game of the ALCS, NLCS, or World Series, any game of the Eastern or Western Conference Finals for both the NBA and NHL, and any game of the Stanley Cup may be granted exemption from Rule 27." She eyes the basket of breadsticks. "This is the first game of the Eastern Conference Finals," she says, pointing over her shoulder at the flat screen, "and, I'll have you know, Boston hasn't reached this far in the playoffs since '93. I should add another addendum that compensates for drought."

The bartender fires up a blender that drowns out what she just said, and Ken knows he should ask her to repeat herself, but Kendra looked awfully agitated while saying it. The blender is loud. It whirls and chops and sounds like a speedboat bouncing off waves. He looks down to her chest.

"Why do they call it motorboating?" he asks.

She pinches the plunge of her pink shirt and hoists it upward. "That's inappropriate conversation. Also, you took two breadsticks."

Ken slouches and returns one of the breadsticks to the basket. Dating is difficult. Kendra turns away again and keeps a steady eye on the Bruins game.

"It's May," he says, to her orange ponytail. "It's too warm for hockey." He plops the rest of his breadstick into his mouth and glances at the basket.

Kendra turns slowly to him with wide eyes. She says nothing. Garlic butter slips in the sweat of Ken's palms, and he nearly coughs on the hunk of dough in his mouth.

"What did you just say?" she asks. He is quiet, shrinking in the intensity of her stare. He shrugs and mumbles something about it being baseball season. She takes the napkin from her lap, crumples it and places it on the table. "This isn't going to happen."

Ken swallows the bread. It drags its heels down his throat. His eyes water and when his voice returns he asks, "Should we go back to Bengy's?"

"I mean us," she says, pointing back and forth between the two of them. "This isn't going to work out."

"Are you breaking up with me?" he asks. She sighs and averts his glance. He shakes his head and whispers, "But I'm paying you."

She frowns and looks apologetically back at him. "I know. That makes this difficult. I can't actually break up with you as we're not actually dating, but I think we should stop seeing each other, if that makes any sense." She fixes a strand of wayward hair behind her pointy ear. "In all my years of coaching, I've never had to break up with a client. I had a one hundred percent success rate before you came along; I placed all my clients with real girlfriends before the six-month mark. But you're a special case, Ken."

"I *am* a special case," he says. He slides the breadstick basket aside and speaks to her in a soft voice. "We can get serious, you and me. You can drop your other clients and we can . . ."

"We can what? Ride off into the sunset and live handsomely off your Rubble Rental pension?" She shushes him when he begins to tell her that he doesn't get a pension. "This will be good for you," she says. She speaks in a sympathetic tone. "I honestly believe you'd be better off by making some necessary changes in your life, Ken. You've never received a promotion and your boss is twenty years younger than you."

"Yeah, but he's over a foot taller."

"And you need some new clothes, and some new friends, or any friends, for that matter, not to sound mean. You need to join a gym, and," she whispers, "you need to wash your sheets once in a while." She sighs and averts eye contact. "I'm sorry. I've said too much." She takes her purse and scoots from the booth.

"We're leaving? We haven't ordered yet."

"I'm leaving, Ken, if you'll excuse me. I'd like to sit at the bar and watch the game, alone." She stands from the booth, smoothes the wrinkles from her blouse and apologizes again. "Take a few weeks, get yourself together, and maybe we'll pick things up from there."

Ken watches her walk away. He watches her slip between the waiters and busboys bustling about with trays of drinks and plates and tubs of dirty dishes. He thinks of returning to his dingy apartment, to his sticky dishes in the sink, to his dirty sheets, to his imprinted seat on the couch, to the television and the radio that fill the silence of his existence. He thinks of stopping her.

He thinks of telling her that he likes her ears. He thinks of telling her that he loves her vocabulary. He thinks of telling her that he loves that she corrects him when he speaks incorrectly. He thinks of telling her that she brings out the best in him. He thinks of telling her that he loves her. Instead, he glimpses her as she takes a seat at the bar. The young, full-haired bartender approaches her with a handsome smile, and the Bruins score, and the crowd erupts in cheers, hundreds of hands in the air. He can no longer see Kendra's orange hair.

THREE

At home, he has another bowl of Rice Krispies for dinner. He sets the bowl of milk on the concrete patio for the stray cat that visits occasionally, and he returns to his grooved imprint on the couch. He spends the evening watching the Bruins and the Lightning skate around in circles. He doesn't understand the appeal of the game. Maybe if they made the nets bigger there would be more scoring. Maybe they should get rid of the goalies altogether. Why does Kendra like this so much?

His front door whips open and Ivan stomps in with the white envelope he uses to collect rent. Ken is too familiar with this routine. Ivan will stand in front of the television, purposely blocking

Ken's view, and he'll dangle the envelope by the masking tape stuck to his thumb, and he'll call Ken a deadbeat, suggest his mother is a harlot who ought to be ashamed of him, and he'll swear in some Slavic language before sticking the envelope to Ken's television screen and slamming the door shut when he storms out.

Ken braces himself as Ivan marches over to the television. But Ivan stops. "You watch the game tonight?" he asks. He sits beside Ken and elbows him in the ribs until he moves over, and he stares straight ahead, transfixed by the game, just as Kendra did earlier in the evening. Who knew hockey was so popular?

Ivan opens his palms to the air and shouts, "Nevedia streliť gól!"

Ken glances cautiously to the

screen and back to his new guest, not knowing what the hell he's just said. "Would you like a drink? I have milk or champagne."

Ivan waves a dismissive hand at him without taking his eyes off the game. Then he squints at Ken. "Šampanského?" he says. "You drink champagne when we lose? The fuck is amatter with you?"

"Well, it was for my girlfriend. But she broke up with me tonight."

"Posrali, Zdeno!" Ivan sinks his face in his hands and grumbles.

"I'll be okay," Ken says, reassuring him. "I guess I should have seen it coming. But I think if I make some necessary changes in my life, she might see that I'm boyfriend material. Maybe even husband material." Ken imagines himself getting down on one knee and wowing Kendra with a shiny diamond, maybe amid the crowd at Stockbridge Tavern, and all their agitated faces suddenly overcome with joy, and all their cheering would be for him and Kendra, and—

"Because you're a pussykitty."

"Pardon?"

Ivan turns away from the television as the clock winds down on the third period. "You're, ako sa vraví, a pushover. She leaves you because you're a pussykitty."

"Oh. I think it's either pussycat or pussy. Usually pussy is more offensive, so . . ."

"See?" Ivan says, whacking him over the head with the rent envelope. "Too nice."

"I'm too nice? Compared to you," Ken says, fixing his hair. "But you're angry most of the time. Some of the time. A lot of the time, maybe."

Ivan smirks. "But I am no failure with woman."

"So you're saying I should be mean? I don't think that'll work."

"Look," Ivan says, pointing to the screen as two Bruins players pick fights in the final seconds of the game. "You think they have trouble with ladies?"

Ken's jaw drops. "Is that allowed? Number eighteen just popped that guy in the face."

"Of course." Ivan laughs and lifts himself off the couch. "Number eighteen married a model. Ladies love hockey."

With that, he tapes the rent envelope to the door and leaves.

The television becomes Ken's only

companion again. He watches the re-
caps of the goals (slap shots and snap
shots and backhanded wrist shots) that
seem so easy. The coverage focuses on the
Bruins' first goal: number nineteen, who
looks a lot like that handsome bartender, sprinting over the blue line, thread-
ing the puck under the defenseman's
reach and shoveling it past the goalten-
der's skate.

"I can do that," Ken thinks.

He looks down at his feet, at his
hands, and he gets up from the couch,
holding an imaginary hockey stick in his
imaginary gloves. He makes a shooting
motion and applauds his own agility.
"Get angry," he tells himself. He drops
his imaginary stick, shakes his imaginary
gloves from his hands, and suddenly he
is the world's best boxer, on skates.

Outside on the patio, the stray cat creeps over to the cereal bowl and sips the milk while keeping an eye on Ken through the sliding screened door.

"Scram!" Ken jumps toward the door, and the cat skitters across the concrete. He watches as the black-and-white fur jounces into the darkness, disappearing, and he thinks, "Oh gosh, that was awful."

"I'm sorry, Mittens," he says, calling through the screen, though he knows the stray doesn't respond to Mittens, or Socks, or Little Buddy. He grabs the box of dry food that he keeps by the door, and steps out to the patio, shaking the box and making kissing sounds, calling the poor thing back.

One of his neighbors tells him to shut the fuck up. Ken bites his lip, clutches the box of cat food to his chest, and back-steps, quietly, into his apartment. He returns to his imprint on the couch, slouches, and calls himself a pussykitty.

FOUR

Eight days and fourteen hundred dollars later, Ken is prepared to play hockey. He's purchased the skates, the shin guards, the jockstrap, the garter belt, the hockey pants, the elbow pads, the gloves, the helmet, the mouth guard, the shoulder pads, and the massive bag in which to haul it all.

His new friend, Kirk (wildcat .captain@30+ice.com), told him to arrive at the rink a half hour before their Sunday night game, which is the only time slot afforded to the 30+ league.

Kirk is a stern-faced man who does not smile when Ken calls him Captain Kirk. "This way," he says, leading Ken through the double doors. But Ken's hockey bag gets lodged in the doorway and jerks him backward. His hands go up and his stick knifes through the air and nearly takes Kirk's ear off.

"Are you new to this?" he asks.

"No," Ken says, adjusting himself and stepping sideways through the door. "Well, yeah, sort of."

"Can you at least skate?" Kirk asks, leading him around the sheet of ice, the outside of the boards, old wood graffitied with initials and team names, the glass with its own graffiti of black flecks—scattered streaks from rough collisions with pucks, sticks, helmets, noses. "'Cause the last guy we had, he couldn't keep himself up and he got wrecked up pretty bad."

Ken laughs a nervous laugh and assures Kirk that he can skate.

But that's a lie. Ken hasn't stood on skates since he was a kid.

Kirk swings the locker room door open to a dozen men in various stages of gearing up—fixing their shin guards over their legs, stretching their socks over their shin guards, clipping their garter belts to their socks, hoisting their pants over their garter belts, tying their pants or tying their skates. Ken gulps. He doesn't even know how to get dressed.

He drops his heavy bag on the matted floor and tosses his stick onto the bag. The blade hits the floor and the stick topples off the bag. His teammates look up from their laces, or down from their shoulder pads, and there is a collective silence as they stare at Ken's stick. Ken catches his breath and worries he's bought a street hockey stick.

Kirk collects the stick from the floor and takes it to the locker room door. "Guys usually keep these outside," he says. He props the door open and leans the stick against the hallway wall in a queue of a dozen other sticks that Ken had walked by without noticing.

"I forgot," Ken says, as if he knew already, as if he hadn't just given himself up for a rookie.

A tall man with missing teeth turns to Kirk and asks him if he still has Dwyer's jersey. "You should give it to the new guy," he says. Ken thinks he's being nice, but the team shares a knowing laugh.

"Aren't we playing the Ice Dogs tonight?" another man asks, and the team laughs again as they return to tying their skates, pants, or jerseys.

Ken unzips his bag. His hands shake as he removes his equipment, piece by piece, and his breathing stutters through his chest. He thinks of walking out. He thinks of returning all this expensive crap. But then he thinks of the snotty clerk at the sporting goods store, how he repeated the return policy so carefully. He thinks of Kendra, how impressed she'll be with him, eventually.

Ken stands from the bench and whisks away his gym pants faster than a trained Chippendales dancer. He glances at the man next to him, who cautiously slides away from Ken on the bench. He's a hefty bald-headed guy with stretched-out tattoos on his arms. He throws a handful of ju-ju-bees in his mouth and chews as he fastens his shin guards in place. Ken memorizes his pattern of dress: shins, socks, pants, skates, shoulders, elbows, jersey, helmet, gloves.

He wrestles with his laces and listens to the typical locker-room banter. The guys make crude remarks about a good-looking lady named Franka, and Ken is reminded of Kendra—women with men's names. The laughter and conversation dies down as more and more guys finish dressing and depart for the ice.

Ken is given a Wildcats jersey and, sure enough, it says "Dwyer" on the back.

"Wear it with pride," the toothless defenseman says as he walks by in his skates, past Ken and out of the locker room.

Ken is the last man dressed. Alone, he musters the courage to finally stand up on his skates. He waddles toward the exit, grips the metal ridge of the door handle with his gloved fingers and stops. He looks up to the dingy ceiling and prays he doesn't get killed out there on the ice.

FIVE

And Ken nearly gets killed out there. First right out of the gate, when he steps onto the sheet of ice and it slips from under him and the rafters spin like the grid of a hamster wheel and Ken lands square on his ass. And, when he can't get up—both because his tailbone rings so

32

badly that his spinal column can't stack and because his skates can't catch an edge on the freshly cleaned ice—he falls again, square on his ass.

Ken lies there on the ice, staring through the cage of his helmet at the rafters and the legs of the other team's players as they step through the gate, hurdle over him, and glide off in perfect strides.

One of the Ice Dogs races toward Ken's recumbent body and stops just short of him, spraying him with snow and water. "You're gonna get it, Dwyer," the man says, jabbing Ken in the ribs with the blade of his stick.

When Ken wipes himself off and finally brings himself up, he remembers what he learned as a kid—lean forward, push off with one skate, then the next—and he is able to make it to the bench, where the rest of the Wildcats, in varying degrees of disappointment, discouragement, and disbelief, collectively shun him.

In the time it took him to fall (twice), to get up, and to glide over to the bench, he's missed warm-ups. The lone referee chirps on his whistle and calls the captains to the face-off circle. Ken sits on the bench and assesses the height of the boards before him. He wonders how he'll hurdle over them and onto the ice.

Kirk is addressing the team, saying something about quick line changes and fresh legs, and something else that makes no sense to Ken. "Dwyer," Kirk says, skating backward from the bench, "replace Dom on defense." Kirk coasts into the face-off circle, bent over, with his stick resting over his thighs.

Ken elbows the tattooed guy next to him. "Which one's Dom?" The man points to the toothless defenseman at the far side of the circle, the one who insisted that Ken wear Dwyer's jersey. Dom smirks at Ken, a toothless smirk, and then a wink. "Oh, God," Ken says. Dwyer could be dead for all he knows.

The whistle chirps again and the referee drops the puck, and sticks collide, and skates chop and slice, and Ken sits on the bench. His tailbone aches. He watches his teammates hustle and glide after the puck, and he keeps an eye on Dom. He skates forward and turns backward in one motion, he drops to his knees and slides along the ice, breaking up a pass with his body, and he jumps to his skates and plays the puck off the boards, sending Kirk through the neutral zone.

"Shit," Ken thinks. "I can't do this." Suddenly he has to pee. He wiggles his knees until the feeling goes away.

The forwards change lines, and fellow Wildcats who sat beside him just moments ago, yelling and cheering, have already hopped over the boards and onto the ice in a flash, like soldiers out of a bunker. There's no way Ken can jump over these boards. He contemplates the gate at the end of the bench. It locks with a metal bar, like a medieval dungeon.

Dom glides over to the bench and hurdles the boards. "You're on. Go. Go. Go."

Ken stutter-steps around him, toward

the door, catching the butt of his stick in Dom's shoulder. Dom curses at him and asks what the fuck he's doing, but Ken is in a hurry to get out there on the ice. The Ice Dogs are coming. They're racing three-on-one over the blue line, and Ken knows if they score it'll be his fault.

He steps out onto the ice and falls again just as the puck carrier arrives. Ken jousts with his stick and trips the Ice Dog, sending him soaring through the air. He lands chest-first on the ice, and the puck shoots into Ken's body. The whistle blows.

The referee, with his arm in the air, skates over to the scorekeeper and calls out, "Two for tripping, number twenty-three, Dwyer."

Ken picks himself up marginally faster than before, and glides marginally faster than before to the penalty box's gate. He has mixed feelings about this—guilt, of course, and relief. A penalty is a handy excuse not to come back out on the ice for two whole minutes.

If only he could figure out how to open the gate.

He tries pushing the penalty box's door. The boards rattle but they don't budge. He tries pulling. He throws his padded hip into it and the door doesn't buckle. Someone from the bench yells to him, telling him to use his stick. He whacks the gap in the glass with his blade, and nothing happens. The referee chirps on his whistle again, warning that they'll be served a bench minor for too many men on the ice, or delay of game, or some sort of infraction. He's not sure, he admits, because he's never encountered this situation.

Finally the scorekeeper, a woman in a hooded sweatshirt, leaves her post and opens the penalty box from the inside.

Ken thanks her.

She smiles up at him and says, "You're not Dwyer."

Ken takes a seat on the wooden bench and catches his breath. She shrugs and returns to the scorekeeper box.

She is the first woman to start a conversation with Ken since Kendra stopped seeing him, but in this anxious and embarrassing moment, Ken hardly notices. And down the row, on the Wildcats' bench, his teammates chuckle into their gloves. Ken has just inadvertently snubbed the woman of their dreams.

SIX

Ivan is waiting with his rent envelope outside Ken's apartment door. When Ken turns the corner hauling his hockey bag and carrying his stick, Ivan bursts out in laughter.

"Look what the pussy dragged in."

Ken sighs and drops his bag at the doorstep. "It's 'cat.' You'll want to use 'cat' in that context."

"You walk funny," Ivan says, pointing to Ken's legs.

Ken huffs. He unlocks his door, swings it open, lifts his hockey bag despite all the sore muscles and stiff vertebrae, and steps inside his dingy apartment. Ivan follows.

"You do all this for a woman?" he asks, and he laughs again.

"I'm thinking of quitting," Ken says. He opens his freezer and removes a frost-bitten package of peas. He places it over the imprint on his couch and sits on top of it, groaning as it crunches beneath his tailbone.

Ivan stands over Ken's hockey bag, nudging it with his foot. "How much does this cost you?"

Ken is quiet. He turns the television on and the picture unfolds to a documentary series on genetics, which was exactly what he was watching before he left for hockey. The monotone voiceover explains the percentages of Irish, Scottish and Jewish people who are redheaded, and Ken almost tears up, thinking of Kendra.

Ivan makes a concerned expression and sticks the rent envelope to the TV.

He tells Ken to pay up or get out, and slams the door when he leaves.

The stray cat mews on the patio.

Ken groans. He doesn't want to get up off this package of peas, and he can't stomach any cereal right now. The cat paws at the glass and meows again. Ken curses. He hoists himself off the couch, waddles to the fridge, sniffs the carton of milk and pours a bit into a clean bowl (his last). He bends to place the bowl on the patio and his back goes out. He falls to his knees, drops the bowl, and teeters to his side. He curls into a fetal position as the spilled milk drips off his arms, into a pool on the concrete.

Mittens licks the milk off Ken's wrists, turning his poo-stained butt in Ken's face as he does so.

In the coming week, Ken sees a masseuse (twice), he spends eleven dollars at the grocery (two cartons of milk, one plastic cat dish, and three packages of frozen peas), he calls Kendra five times (two hang-ups and three voicemails), he watches eight instructional Internet videos (four how-to-skate, three how-to-stop, and one how-to-get-her-to-respond-to-a-voicemail), and he tunes in for three playoff games without dozing through any of them.

For the next Wildcats game, he is recuperated and invigorated on all those how-to videos. He might be able to skate, he probably won't be able to stop, but Kendra might show up because he left her a detailed voicemail and repeated the time and place and assured her that she'll be pleasantly surprised.

She'll be shocked to see him geared up and playing hockey. He'd better bring his A game.

SEVEN

He is greeted in the locker room by silence, which Kendra would classify as awkward.

"I didn't think you'd show," one teammate tells him.

Ken laughs it off and tells him that he didn't have anything else lined up for the night.

The locker-room antics continue with teasing over the woman named Franka, and crude jokes about librarians and strippers, and librarian strippers. Soon enough, most of the guys finish dressing and depart for the ice. Ken is left with Dom, the toothless defenseman.

Dom clears his throat and, in an unusually soft voice, he asks him, "So what did Franka say to you last week?"

"Who?" Ken asks, plucking desperately at the back of his jersey, trying to free it from where it's stuck on his shoulder pad.

"Franka," Dom says, "the scorekeeper."

Ken's eyes widen. Finally he's in on a locker-room joke. He tries to remember what it was that she said to him as Dom helps him with his jersey, tugging it violently free.

"It was about Dwyer," Ken says, catching his balance. "I think she thought I was him."

Dom chuckles and leaves the locker room before Ken can muster the courage to ask him, "Who the hell is Dwyer?"

Out on the ice, Ken skates a bit better. He's able to glide up and down the sheet and stop with help from the boards. He's also able to get on and off the ice without falling, which is, in his mind, a huge improvement, even if he can't convince any of his teammates to pass him the puck.

The other team spends a disproportionate amount of time covering him. Though it's a no-checking league, they push, elbow and jostle him into the boards. They heckle and taunt and make insulting comments about Dwyer's mother. He spends most of the game picking himself up off the ice.

When he's on the bench, he glances up at the stands for Kendra. But the bleachers remain empty through the entire game, just as they had last week.

He follows his teammates off the ice and into the locker room, and he wonders if Kendra misheard him on the voicemail. Maybe he accidentally gave her the wrong time. Had he said ten o'clock or eleven? What if she shows up at eleven, and he's already gone? She'll think he's standing her up. "Oh, God," Ken says, looking up from untying his skates.

His teammates don't notice him, thankfully. They chat on about the other team, about the referee, about the beers in Dom's Jeep.

An invitation for a drink in the parking lot would be the perfect way to bide some time waiting for Kendra. And if she sees him with his new friends, she'll be even more impressed.

Ken wastes some time getting out of his gear as slowly as he can, but his teammates pack up their bags and saunter out of the locker room, one after the other, without asking him to join them for a beer.

The door closes behind them, and he sits on the bench alone, just as he sits on his own couch every night, alone. He rests his head against the concrete wall of the locker room. He regrets joining this team, buying all this gear, and embarrassing himself in this big, stupid attempt to be something he's not. He should have just stayed home where he belongs.

Just as he lets out a whimpering sigh,

the door opens. A soft voice says, "Oh, Jesus, I'm sorry."

Ken looks up too late. The door is already swinging closed.

Maybe it was Kendra.

He jumps to his feet and darts across the locker room. He whips the door open and hurries into the hall. But there is no one there.

He retrieves his bag and stick from the locker room and walks through the rink, checking the stands one last time for Kendra. Nothing.

Outside in the parking lot, his teammates gather by Dom's Jeep. In the glow of headlights they are taller, stronger, scarier shadows of themselves, standing around, sipping from beers, laughing at jokes that might or might not be about him.

Ken drops his bag on the curb by the rink's entrance and stands over it. He props the butt end of his stick on the pavement and leans on the blade. He scans the lot for Kendra's car. He checks the time and wonders how late she might show up if he told her the wrong time. He fiddles with his cell phone and wishes he had someone to call to make himself look busy. He wishes he had a cigarette to smoke. He should take up smoking, for times like these.

The rink's lights go out behind him.

The door opens and Franka the score-keeper walks out. She squints at Ken and hooks her brown hair behind her ear. "I'm sorry for barging in on you," she says. Ken looks baffled. She thumbs over her shoulder. "In the locker room? Just two minutes ago?"

"That was you?" he asks.

She nods. "I have to make sure they're empty before I lock the doors for the night. Usually they're clear well before eleven o'clock, but good thing I checked or you'd be locked in there all night."

Distracted by a car whizzing by, Ken doesn't respond, and an awkward silence ensues.

"I'm Franka by the way," she says.

"I know."

"Oh, you know?" She laughs, but Ken is busy watching the road for Kendra's car. "Are you waiting for a ride too?" she asks.

Ken shakes his head. "My ex-girlfriend was supposed to show up. But

I told her the wrong time and she's almost always late, so . . ."

Franka nods toward the far end of the parking lot. "You could grab a drink with the guys while you wait."

"They're not really my type," he says.

Franka laughs. For a moment, Ken is sure she's laughing at him, because most times when people laugh around him, it's at his expense. He can't remember the last time he made anyone laugh. He glances over at his teammates in the far corner of the lot. Even in the darkness he can tell he's caught their attention.

"They're not exactly my type either," Franka says.

Ken tries to think of something else to say, because it would be perfect if Kendra pulls up and finds him talking with another woman. He thinks of asking Franka for the score of the game, but he should probably know that information and she probably doesn't care. He thinks of telling Franka about his breakup with Kendra, but he might divulge that Kendra's a "coach" and that will be embarrassing for him and frightening for her, and if she backs away from him, his teammates will *really* have a laugh. And in the time it's taken him to think all this, another awkward silence has ensued. Shit. "Think, think, think," he says to himself.

Headlights glare from the road and blind him as they approach. Ken squints at the car which appears to be a sedan, and red, and Kendra's, but it's not.

"Here's my sister," Franka says, hoisting her purse over her shoulder. "Ten minutes late, as usual." She steps off the curb as the Honda pulls up beside her. She swings the passenger door open and waves to him. "Goodnight, Dwyer."

"Wait," he calls out. He tosses his stick aside and it clanks against the pavement. He hustles off the curb and bends beside the Honda.

Franka rolls the window down and bites her bottom lip in a bewildered expression.

"I just have to ask you something," he says, and he peeks over at her sister and excuses himself for interrupting. He peers through the driver-side window at his teammates across the lot and whispers, "Why do they call me Dwyer?"

Franka laughs. "He's just a guy who used to play in this league. He went from team to team without once playing for a season. He even suckered the Wildcats into getting him a jersey. And now you're wearing his jersey."

Ken nods. "Are they on to me?" he asks. Franka clicks her seatbelt in place and assures him that the other teams will probably gun for him until they realize he's not Dwyer. "No, I mean the Wildcats," Ken says, cocking his head toward the corner of the lot. His teammates have gone silent, and he can almost feel their eyes on him.

"I'm sure they are," she says, smiling at him.

But this sort of flirtation is lost on Ken. Even as the Honda pulls away from the curb and he waves goodbye in the fog of its exhaust, he is thinking of driving past Kendra's condo tonight.

EIGHT

Driving a rental makes stalking less stressful—not that Ken is accustomed to stalking. He dips in the driver's seat and occasionally glances up at the pale glow of Kendra's bay window. Several minutes pass by without the slightest sign of life, and Ken considers leaving.

Then Kendra appears at the kitchen table with her laptop. Ken imagines she's tallying her weekly figures in that complex spreadsheet she built from scratch. Soon enough, this gets incredibly boring, and Ken considers leaving, again.

Then a shirtless man saunters into the kitchen and pulls the refrigerator door open. Ken's breathing halts in his chest.

He reverses out of the parking lot and

speeds home where he'll lie in bed and obsess over the following information:

- Kendra doesn't allow clients to spend the night at her place;
- but Kendra doesn't have any brothers or male family members who might help themselves into her fridge, shirtless;
- also, Ivan left two envelopes taped to the television screen, and that's peculiar;
- but Kendra doesn't see clients on Sunday nights;
- but it's not like she has any bodyguards;
- also, Ivan must really want his rent;
- but maybe she does have a bodyguard . . . it makes sense, given her line of work.

He concludes that, in the event the man actually *is* her boyfriend, it's not the end of the world because he's not particularly attractive, or muscular, or young. In fact, the shirtless man looked a lot like Ken, and for this reason, he decides there's still hope, and he's able to sleep the night through.

At work, Ken is reprimanded for returning rentals that smell bad. His boss, a sharp-looking twenty-something, lifts the trunk of the Mustang and gags. "Jesus, Ken," he says, waving his long arm through the air. "What is that stench? It smells like death and cheese."

Ken knows that the smell of his hockey bag (his sweat and body odor) has seeped into the car's fabric—probably permanently—but he can't bring himself to admit it, and his pay is docked the vacuuming and shampooing expenses.

"I don't know what or who you killed in there," his boss says, "but don't do it again."

At home, Ken gets three, four, five digits through Kendra's phone number and hangs up. He drafts an e-mail and deletes it. He writes a hand-written note and rips it up.

He locks his door and pretends to sleep when Ivan knocks, rings the bell twenty-seven times, and hollers Russian or Slovak swearwords at him.

He cleans himself up and visits the Stockbridge Tavern and orders a soda from the handsome bartender. He hopes Kendra will show up as the bar becomes more and more crowded with Bruins fans who gather in the standing room behind him and bump into him as if he's in the front row of a concert. He searches the crowd for Kendra, glancing over his shoulder more times than at the television.

The bartender suggests he visit Bengy's if he's going to drink soda all night. "They might even throw a scoop of ice cream in it for ya," he says. A few drunken patrons chuckle at that. The bartender fills another glass from the tap and says, "But you'll have to order off the kids' menu."

Ken can't think of a decent comeback, so he leaves without tipping.

Ten o'clock rolls around on Sunday night, and Ken considers calling Kirk and lying about an injury or a death in the family as an excuse to skip hockey and stay in for the night. But Ivan pounds at the door and threatens to barge in, regardless if Ken's "busy whacking it." So Ken sneaks out the sliding door, past the stray cat's bowl, down the hill, around the building and into his rental, a pickup truck, which is perfect for carting his hockey bag around, sans stench.

He is late for hockey. Most of the Wildcats and Lawyers (sponsored by the Law Offices of Everett and Worth) are already skating their pregame drills. The only guys still in the locker room (Dom and two wings) are dressed already. They discuss the opposing goalie's weak glove and strong blocker.

"Go fivehole or gloveside shelf," Dom says. He makes a concerned expression, tosses his helmet on the floor and admits to having had chimichangas for lunch. He waddles in his skates around the tiled half-wall and into the bathroom.

The wingers chuckle as the bathroom stall slams shut. They go on talking about winning offensive face-offs and screening the goalie for Dom's shot from the point, but Dom cannot hear them.

"Is there anyone out there?" he calls from the bathroom. "There's no toilet paper in here."

Ken and the wingers exchange troubled glances.

"Guys? You there?" Dom says. His pleading echoes off the tiles like that of a child stuck in a well. The wingers chuckle silently and sneak out of the locker room, closing the door softly behind them.

"Hello? Anyone?"

Ken closes his eyes and breathes for a moment. The stench radiating from the stall is suffocating, and knowing the beany and deep-fried burritoey source makes it worse. Without announcement, Ken goes to the opposite stall, unhinges the toilet paper and hands it under the partition, safely into Dom's waiting palm.

Ken wants to be dressed and out of the locker room before Dom returns from the bathroom, but Dom shows just as Ken secures his helmet on his head. He waddles to the locker room exit without saying anything to Ken, and Ken is fine with that. Kendra would tell him it's "man code" not to acknowledge moments of compassion or, as she would put it, "lapses in male detachment." But

Dom surprises him. He looks over his bulky shoulder pad and, in a voice deeper than his normal speaking tone, he says, "This never happened." He swings the locker room door open and waddles out.

Ken decides he can't win at anything. Out on the ice, he trips the first Lawyer who calls him Dwyer, and lands himself in the penalty box.

He hangs his head and studies the mess of spit and gum and Gatorade stains on the penalty box floor. He listens to the scuff and scrape of skates, the click of the puck ricocheting off the glass, the rumble of the boards as wooden and composite sticks chop at the puck in the corners, and he wonders who the hell chews gum while playing hockey. Don't these guys believe in mouth guards? Then it occurs to him that—oh God—he's the only one wearing a mouth guard.

He unsnaps his helmet and whips it off his head. He sets it on the floor and unclasps the rubber strip that attaches his mouth guard to his cage like a yellow ribbon strung to a child's binky. He takes the mouth guard by the strip and flings it to the corner of the penalty box. He returns his helmet to his head and prays that no one saw that.

In the scorekeeper box beside him, Franka tries to get his attention, but he can't hear her until she taps on the glass. She smiles wide at him and points to the stands. "Is that your girlfriend?" she asks, shouting through the glass.

Ken's eyes dart to the bleachers, but the lone spectator is not Kendra. A woman with dark hair fidgets with her cell phone and takes very little interest in her boyfriend or husband's hockey game.

Ken shakes his head at Franka. "She has red hair."

Franka laughs and says something that sounds like "ginger beave," but Ken doesn't take her for the kind of person who would freely inquire about the color of a woman's pubes. But when he asks her to repeat herself, he hears the same syllables. He tries to sort it out. Not gin, but juice? Something juice, juice? Then he remembers the documentary he watched on redheads and it all makes sense.

"No," he says. "I'm pretty sure she's Catholic."

Franka's eyebrows raise, then they buckle in a concerned expression just as Ken's two minutes expire.

He steps back to the ice and closes the door of the penalty box behind him. Before he can turn to the bench, a Lawyer shouts out an obscenity meant for Dwyer.

Ken stiffens when he hears the name, and sure enough, he is crosschecked from behind. He smacks into the boards right in front of Franka's scorekeeper box. His facemask collides with the hard shelf of the boards, and he hits the ice like a dropped marionette, crumpled in a heap of twisted limbs.

When he opens his eyes he thinks he sees the Power Rangers standing over him. Franka snaps her fingers just above the cage of his facemask and he finds her kneeling on the ice. His teammates hover over him in a half-circle.

"What the hell is stuck to his helmet?" one of the Wildcats asks. "Is that gum?"

"I think it's a ju-ju-bee," Franka says. "Someone had a feast of them on the visitor's bench and in the penalty box, and in the locker room."

Ju-ju-bee, Ken thinks, not "ginger beave." Then it occurs to him, because his mind is still mushy, that he's said this last part out loud.

His teammates laugh. But behind the row of teammates hovering over him, a scuffle starts. Dom shouts and drops his gloves and goads a Lawyer to come at him. He shoves him in the shoulder, but the refs intervene and escort Dom and the Lawyer to their respective benches before any roughing penalties can be dished out.

Ken insists that he's fine. He gets to his feet with little assistance and takes a seat on the bench. His ribcage aches. It hurts to breathe, to expand his chest and draw in new air.

Down the row, Dom berates a teammate for not retaliating for Ken, for not taking care of his own. He keeps a careful eye on the Lawyers' bench and times his line change just right. When the offending Lawyer switches up, Dom hops over the boards and levels him at center ice. He stands over the Lawyer and shouts, "Stop calling him Dwyer."

On the bench, the Wildcats stand and clank their sticks against the boards as Dom is escorted off the ice and kicked out of the game. Captain Kirk skates to the bench, uncaps a water bottle and tells Ken, "We gotta get you a new jersey."

NINE

After the game, he is invited to have a beer with the guys in the parking lot, and despite an intolerable headache, Ken agrees. He can't refuse the offer, now that he's finally feeling included.

He gets drunk quickly, too quickly, on account of a likely head injury. The pavement wavers beneath him and the headlights sway like ghosts across the parking lot, and his teammates' voices echo on and on as if Ken's head is empty. He laughs at jokes he doesn't get, and he listens to stories about people he doesn't know, but he feels great. Dom wraps an arm around Ken's shoulders and toasts to his new jersey, though he suggests they simply place masking tape over Dwyer with Ken's name.

Ken laughs, but Dom is serious.

Eventually the guys finish their last beers and they take off in their cars or SUVs or trucks and they go home to their wives or girlfriends or roommates, and Ken is the last one left, sitting in his rental pickup, waiting out his buzz.

It feels great to be part of the team, finally, but without Kendra, he still feels empty.

He reclines in the driver's seat and listens to his soft rock and tries to focus on the orange lights that appear to square dance around the console—the check engine light in a do-si-do with the battery light—and he drifts off into a dream about a wrecking ball, his apartment wall, Mittens and a bowl of milk.

What feels like twenty seconds is, in fact, fifty minutes. He awakes to a tapping on his window. Franka's sister peeks through the glass. The Honda's headlights burn behind her and Ken can barely make out Franka, leaning on the open passenger door, her chin resting in her crossed arms.

Her sister motions for him to roll down the window, but in his sleepy stupor, he can't figure out the window lock. She swings his door open, and he falls out, hitting the pavement much as he hit the ice earlier in the night.

"I think you need a ride home," she says.

In the backseat of the Honda, Ken goes on about Mittens and he stresses how thankful he is for the ride home because Mittens is probably hungry, and even though Mittens is not his cat, and not officially named Mittens, he thinks of Mittens as his pet and his responsibility because someone clearly abandoned him, and some people shouldn't be allowed to have pets since they just toss them out on their own as soon as they claw the couch, or poop outside the litter box, or something.

In between this spewing monologue, Franka's sister asks simple left or right questions, but otherwise guesses her way to Ken's apartment. And Ken cannot tell, in his inebriated state, that Franka, who gazes back at him from the front seat, is taken by his concern for the stray.

When he arrives home he finds a notice to vacate signed, "Regrettabally, Ivan." He tugs the note from where it's taped to his door and drags himself inside his dingy apartment. He goes to the sliding door, hauls it open and scoops Mittens from the patio. He scatters cat food on the living room floor, and he passes out on the couch.

He dreams of a party, a bachelor party, though it's not his own, and a limo. He and his teammates drink and laugh and pose for pictures, but a giant feather duster tickles him and his face twitches in every frame. He awakes to the cat sleeping on his head. And the phone. His phone is ringing. Franka says she's on her way to pick him up, to drive him to the rink, to get his truck back.

"Already?" he asks, squinting at the

cable box for the time. It's half past eight. His stomach grumbles and his head spins, but all he can think about is Ivan's eviction notice. He hangs up with Franka and doesn't bother to get dressed in cleaner clothes, or to brush his teeth, or to pat down his hair.

Outside, he plods down the stairs, along the walkway and out to the parking lot where Franka idles in the Honda. He plops himself into the passenger seat and thanks her for picking him up.

She wears a brown cardigan, and glasses, and her hair in a bun. She pulls away from the curb as Ken draws his seatbelt over his torso. She glances over at him. "What's wrong?" she asks.

And she asks this in such a natural tone, as if they're friends, as if they've been friends for years and she can tell, by the very way he reaches for his seatbelt, that he is upset. He draws a deep breath and tells her, "I missed rent. Twice. I stupidly spent all my money on hockey and I can't afford to pay rent, and my landlord wants to evict me and I thought he was my friend."

Franka apologizes for his misfortune and suggests he return all the equipment. But Ken wouldn't get half as much money in return for his gear, and he's actually starting to enjoy playing hockey, or at least being on the team. He recalls his dream last night, how he and the guys spilled their drinks in the limo and shared an appetizer platter. Why did they have nachos in the limo?

"What about work?" Franka asks, pulling up to a stop sign. "Are you working full-time?"

"Yes," Ken says, snapped from his reverie, "but I don't make very much, even though I've worked there forever."

Franka nudges her glasses upward over the bridge of her nose. "You should demand a raise. My sister is a manager at her office and she takes all these 'Women in the Workplace' seminars. She says that men receive raises when they ask to be rewarded, not necessarily when they wait to be rewarded."

Ken wonders if she is judging his manhood, like Ivan and Kendra and all those guys who called him Dwyer. An awkward silence makes the tolling of the Honda's left-turn signal sharply noticeable. "I get it," Ken says, sounding more annoyed than he intends to. "I should stop being such a wimp and man up about everything."

Franka sighs. "It's not about being a tough guy," she says. "It's about being assertive. If you've been working there a long time, you're certainly justified in asking for a raise. You ought to march into your boss's office and tell him you think it's time already. How else are you going to pay your rent?"

Ken looks over at her as she pulls into the rink parking lot. Even in her dark glasses and bun and ugly cardigan she is distinctly pretty, all cheekbones and freckles and glasses.

"Why are you dressed like a librarian?" he asks. He is aware of his brashness only after the question has left his lips.

"Because I'm a librarian," she says with a smirk that develops into a smile. She laughs as she parks beside his pickup truck. He recalls the librarian jokes that the guys made in the locker room, and he thinks better than to mention it. He doesn't go along with that stuff anyways.

He thanks her again for the ride, and for being so nice to him despite his rudeness, his drunkenness, and his probable smelliness, which he cannot detect but can assume is quite potent.

She smiles over at him. "Anytime, my friend."

TEN

Ken doesn't bite his fingernails when he's nervous. Instead he bites at the fine hairs on the back of his fingers and rips them away with his teeth. He spends the morning doing this behind the counter at Rubble Rental. Between customers, he closes his eyes and softly recites his long list of reasons why he's due for a raise.

But just before lunch, when he finds himself filling the space of his boss's office door and saying "um" way too many times, and panicking, he forgets his list. He remembers Franka telling him to march into that office and tell his boss already.

His six-foot-seven and twenty-something-year-old boss stands from his desk chair and secures the top button of his suit jacket. And Ken, some eleven inches shorter, straightens his stance and says, "I think it's time for a raise. That's all."

To his surprise, his boss nods. He taps his slender, silver pen on his blotter and says, "I don't disagree, Ken. I'll certainly see to it."

By the end of the day, Ken has

verification of a seven and a half percent raise beginning with next week's
paycheck.

He can't wait to get home and call Kendra. If she wasn't impressed that he's playing hockey and making new friends, she'll
surely be impressed now that he's earned
himself a raise. He's made all the "necessary changes" she listed out for him. She
might have said something about a gym
membership, but the hockey should suf-
fice, and something about doing laundry, or changing his sheets, but there's
still time. He's even taken on the responsibility of a new pet, Mittens . . . who
has very likely pooped on the floor in
the time Ken's been at work.

He speeds home, races through the
parking lot, up the stairs, down the hall,

and swings his apartment door open to find Ivan sitting on his couch with Mittens curled on his lap. Ken's last carton of milk lies on the coffee table, its spout unfolded. "You have nice TV," Ivan says, petting Mittens, "and very nice pussy, but no good beer."

Ken runs his hand over his thinning hair and sets his car keys on the end table. "I get it," he says. "I haven't paid rent, so technically you live here. This is *your* TV, *your* cat, *your* empty carton of milk. I get it."

"Do I have popcorn?" Ivan asks. "I eat popcorn when I watch hockey."

Ken unfolds a bag of popcorn and sets it in the microwave. "Did the cat poop on the floor while I was out?" he asks over the racket of kernels popping.

"Yes," Ivan says without turning from

the TV. "Very smelly. I pick up and flush it down the drain."

Ken isn't sure if he means the toilet or the disposal. He cautiously glances at the dishes in his kitchen sink and decides not to investigate. "That was nice of you," he says.

He takes the bag of popcorn to the couch and sits beside Ivan, who refuses to slide down so as not to disturb the sleeping cat on his lap. And the two of them sit shoulder to shoulder on the ratty couch, waiting for game three of the Stanley Cup to start.

"I have some good news," Ken says. He clears his throat and explains his recent victory at work. "If you can bear with me until next week," he says between bites of his fingers, "I'll be able to pay rent for both this month and last."

Ivan is quiet. He pets Mittens and listens to him purr. He looks up at Ken and says, "I like you. And I like your cat."

"You can't have my cat," Ken says, opening the bag of popcorn and letting the steam escape.

"The TV?" Ivan asks.

Ken thinks about it. He could probably do without a television. He thinks of what he could get done around the apartment—laundry, dishes, vacuuming, poop scooping—if he didn't waste so much time watching music videos and weird documentaries. "You can have the TV," he says.

Ivan nods. "We win tonight," he says, pointing to the game, "then I take your TV."

"But I just said you can have it."

Ivan grabs a fistful of popcorn and

explains, "We win tonight, you pay me rent, you stay here, and I take your TV."

"Okay, fine," Ken says, and the two of them sit uncomfortably close, share the popcorn and stare at the television, transfixed by the game.

With each shot on net, popcorn bursts from Ivan's grip and scatters to the floor like a fizzled firework. He swears in whatever language he speaks and throws his hands in the air. Mittens glares up at him, yawns, stretches, and moves to Ken's lap, and Ken plucks pieces of popcorn from his fur.

As Boston takes the lead just eleven seconds into the second period, Ivan leaps from the couch and dances around the coffee table. Ken laughs, watching him celebrate. He laughs harder when

Ivan dances another three times before the period is through.

Just weeks ago Ken would cringe at the sound of Ivan's accent, but now he hopes Ivan won't take off early since Boston has a cushioned lead going into the third. And Ivan doesn't. In fact, he stays another hour after the game, celebrating, talking strategy and watching post-game coverage.

"I suppose you can take the television with you," Ken says when Ivan goes to the door.

Ivan shakes his head. "I keep it here," he says. "My wife, she talks for entire game."

Ken nods and wishes his new friend goodnight. He feeds Mittens and decides to call Kendra.

He is not surprised when she doesn't

answer, and he is not let down. For the first time, he doesn't care. "Home ice seems to be the factor," he says to her voicemail. "I'm worried Vancouver will take the cup on one-goal wins at home."

Just as he hangs up, his phone rings. It's Kendra.

"Ken?" she says. "Ken, did you see that game? Wasn't it amazing?"

He concurs. "Yes, it was."

"Ken, I'm sorry I haven't called. It's just that I've taken time off work to watch all the games and I've still been so busy. But I got all your messages. How's hockey going?"

Ken tells her about his adventures on the ice, omitting certain details about Dwyer, and falling, and hitting his head hard enough to black out. "My puck-handling skills aren't up to snuff," he says, "so I try not to carry the puck too often."

"It's *stick*-handling skills," she says. "But you'll get there. You just have to be in the right place. Play the puck behind the net to the other defender, or play it high off the glass to one of the wingers. If you have to carry it yourself, just get to the red line and dump it in. Let the other guys chase it."

Ken doesn't quite understand this, but he thanks her nonetheless for her help, and a silence ensues.

"I think they're gonna win it," she says. "It's not just tonight's game; I really believe they can win the cup. I have such hope, Ken."

Another silence befalls them and Ken

considers asking her if she still has hope in him, but he decides against it.

"If the invitation still stands," she says, "I'd love to see one of your games."

ELEVEN

Ken gets to the rink an hour and a half before his game and watches the early match between the Ice Dogs and the Lawyers. He sits in the stands and spaces out as his eyes follow the puck from end to end. If he had a natural hockey sense, he'd scout the other teams' defensive strategies, pinpoint their weaknesses and report back to Captain Kirk. But he doesn't.

He thinks about Kendra showing up to the game tonight and his stomach jostles about. He really can't skate all that well, and he still can't stop, and his teammates have never passed him the puck.

Franka waves from the scorekeeper's box.

Ken climbs down the stands and strolls around the outside of the boards to her post. She leans backward in her chair and peeks up at him over her shoulder. "You're here early," she says.

"My ex-girlfriend is coming to the game tonight and I'm nervous as all hell."

She waves her hand through the air and tells him he has nothing to worry about. "I'm sure she'll be so impressed."

"I don't know," Ken says. "She gave me all these instructions on what to do, where to be, and how to carry the puck to the red line, and I still can't skate with it."

Franka sighs. "If she's going to judge you on your stick-handling skills, she doesn't deserve you." The whistle blows and Franka presses a button on her keyboard to stop the game clock.

"Personally," she says, "I think you can do better."

The referee skates over and bends before the glass. "Number eight with the goal, and . . ."

"Twenty-two with the assist," Franka says, marking it down on carbon paper. The referee skates back to center ice and Franka waits for him to drop the puck at the face-off circle before she can start the game clock again. And Ken waits. The puck seems to take forever to fall, as if in slow motion, saucering to the ice between the crouched centers with their blades jousting for position, and Ken doesn't know what to say.

He has never thought of himself as particularly deserving of a woman's attention. He has spent his whole life fighting for approval, trying to be funny, trying to sound smart, trying to act tough. If he were all these things (and perhaps a bit more cleanly and wealthy), Kendra would accept him as boyfriend material. She would appreciate him. She would love him.

Franka peeks over her shoulder at him again. "I'm sorry," she says. "I shouldn't have said that. It's not my business."

On the opposite side of the ice, Ken's teammates file into the rink. They carry their bags into the locker room and motion to him. Ken nods. "I should go."

His teammates cheer for him when he enters the locker room. Ken is baffled by the applause and, for a moment, he looks over his shoulder for someone famous.

Kirk tosses him a new Wildcats jersey. "You're no longer Dwyer," he says.

Ken unfolds it, and there on the back is his name in white block letters: KEN. He chuckles and tells them how nice the jersey looks. His teammates get back to business, unzipping their hockey bags and unloading their equipment. "But shouldn't it say my last name?" he asks.

"No one knew your last name," Kirk says, squelching a strip of Velcro free from his shin guard.

Ken sits on the locker-room bench and drapes the jersey over his lap. He traces the letters of his name with his index finger in a wistful rhythm. He closes his eyes and listens to the sounds of his teammates fastening tape around their socks, tugging the laces of their skates, snapping their facemasks into place, and he tries to memorize the sounds, the sound of the locker-room door squealing open and knocking to a close, the sound of his teammates waddling by in the shuffle of hockey pants, and the sound of their voices. "You ready Ken? You don't want to keep the scorekeeper waiting."

He rests his head against the concrete wall and remembers the last time he sat here, alone, sulking and wishing he had stayed home, when Franka walked in on him.

He breathes in the smell of hockey gear and sweat and faint bleach, and he tells himself to always remember what this moment feels like.